The author is retired and came to writing late in life. Although he has lived his adult years in the South of England, this story however has North of England ethos, reflecting his upbringing and his spiritual home. The story, originally intended to entertain his grandchildren, is not seeking to inculcate any deep moral values but rather to amuse and perhaps even to encourage an occasional 'kick against the pricks' of conformity. He too was once an 'Albert'.

A Visit to the ZOO

Lister Fielding

AUSTIN MACAULEY PUBLISHERS™
LONDON * CAMBRIDGE * NEW YORK * SHARJAH

ISBN 9781528936446 (Paperback)
ISBN 9781528968706 (ePub e-book)

www.austinmacauley.com

First Published (2021)
Austin Macauley Publishers Ltd
25 Canada Square
Canary Wharf
London
E14 5LQ

To Lucy Rankin, my niece, who loves zoos.

Albert was known to be naughty
By everybody at school.
He wasn't malign or vindictive
But he repeatedly broke every rule.

The headmaster called in his mother
To try and make Albert conform
And his mother spoke to him sternly
But it didn't make him reform.

It was coming to that time of the year
When the school's zoo trip would depart.
They told Albert he wouldn't be going
Without a real change of heart.

To everyone's utter surprise
This seemed to get Albert's attention.
He ceased to need reprimanding
And he stopped being put in detention.

The day of the zoo trip arrived
And the staff all together concluded
That Albert was now in the clear
And thoroughly deserved being included.

As the children boarded the coach
They received a packed lunch for the day.
They all had come with their satchels
And they all packed their lunches away.

When the school arrived at the zoo
A special treat had been planned.
They were brought to the penguin enclosure
To feed fish to the penguins by hand.

While Albert joined in at first
He quickly seemed to lose heart.
He broke off from feeding the penguins
And clutching his bag, drew apart.

It was one of those rare summer days
When the weather was sunny and fine.
The children saw all of the creatures
And had such a wonderful time.

Just one boy was missing the fun
Young Albert sat quietly alone,
When a teacher asked, 'Are you all right?'
Albert said, 'Sir, I just want to go home.',

All good things must come to an end,
Time came for the coach to depart
And Albert was first to get on it,
Impatient the journey should start.

When the coach returned to the school
Albert was first to alight.
He thanked the teachers politely and left,
Clutching his satchel quite tight.

His mother had tea on the table.
'Have you had a nice day?' Mother said.
'Yes, Mum but the lunch has upset me.
I need to go lie down in bed.'

As mother cleared the tea all uneaten
Someone at the door rang the bell.
It turned out to be Albert's teacher
Who was worried the lad wasn't well.

'Well thank you for calling,' said mother
'He hasn't eaten his tea.
He didn't even take off his satchel,
Or switch on his favourite TV.'

'Perhaps you should just go and check him.'
Said the teacher, showing concern.
'We don't want the boy to be poorly,
And miss the rest of the term.'

So, taking the advice of the teacher,
Albert's mum up the stairs quietly crept,
Hoping to ask Albert how he was feeling
But not to disturb if he slept.

She opened the door to his bedroom
And Albert was sat on the bed
And sitting beside him, a penguin
Gobbling down the lunch he'd been fed.

So astonished and shocked was poor mother
She emitted a very loud shriek,
Which served only to frighten the penguin,
Who gave her a peck with its beak.

At the sound of her cries, Albert's teacher
Ascended the stairs in a hurry,
Which further upset the penguin
And it flew round the room in a flurry.

Clearly the penguin wasn't house trained
Or perhaps it wasn't used to the bread.
Whichever it was didn't matter because
It kept doing a poop on the bed.

Downstairs, back in the front parlour
The adults held a council of war.
They agreed that the bird must go back to the zoo,
It couldn't stay here anymore!

They contacted the zoo with a phone call.
The night keeper answered the phone.
He explained they'd no overnight transport,
They'd just have to cope on their own.

'Baby Penguins need fish every hour,'
The keeper explained patiently.
'He's in your care and mustn't be harmed,
Or you'll hear from the RSPB.'

'You'd best put the bird in the bathroom,'
Was the keeper's continued advice,
'And if you want him to stay out of trouble,
You should fill up the bath with crushed ice.'

Mother went to look in the larder
To find sardines and salmon in tins,
Whilst the teacher set off to late night shopping
To buy all he could find that had fins.

Now all that a penguin ingests
It seemingly quickly divests
Producing guano might well please a farmer
But it made poor mother depressed.

You can guess that the night went quite slowly,
They took turns for the bird to be fed.
It crunched on crushed ice and ate fish by the slice
Whilst Albert slept soundly in bed.

Albert wasn't so tranquil next morning,
Once the penguin was back in the zoo
Mother borrowed the belt from his teacher
And smacked him quite black and blue.

The teacher had never used violence.
Corporal punishment, surely, was bad?
So how did he think of Mum's conduct?
To be honest, he felt rather glad!